Regan, Mary
French Family.—(Beans)
1. Family—France—Rennes—Juvenile literature
I. Title II. Fairclough, Chris III. Series
306.8'54'094415 HQ624

ISBN 0-7136-2216-4

A&C Black (Publishers) Limited
35 Bedford Row, London WC1R 4JH

Acknowledgments
The map is by Tony Garrett

Filmset by August Filmsetting, Warrington, Cheshire.
Printed in Hong Kong by Dai Nippon Printing Co. Ltd.

French Family

Mary Regan
Photographs by Chris Fairclough

Adam & Charles Black · London

The Gué family live in Rennes, a city in north-west France.
Rennes is the capital of Ille et Vilaine, one of the four *departments* in the *region* of Brittany. The other departments in Brittany are called Finistère, the Côtes du Nord and the Morbihan. France is divided into 95 departments.

Rennes is a very old city. In the city-centre, where Monsieur Gué works, there are cobbled streets and houses built with wooden beams. But towards the outskirts of the city, there are many modern shops, offices and houses.

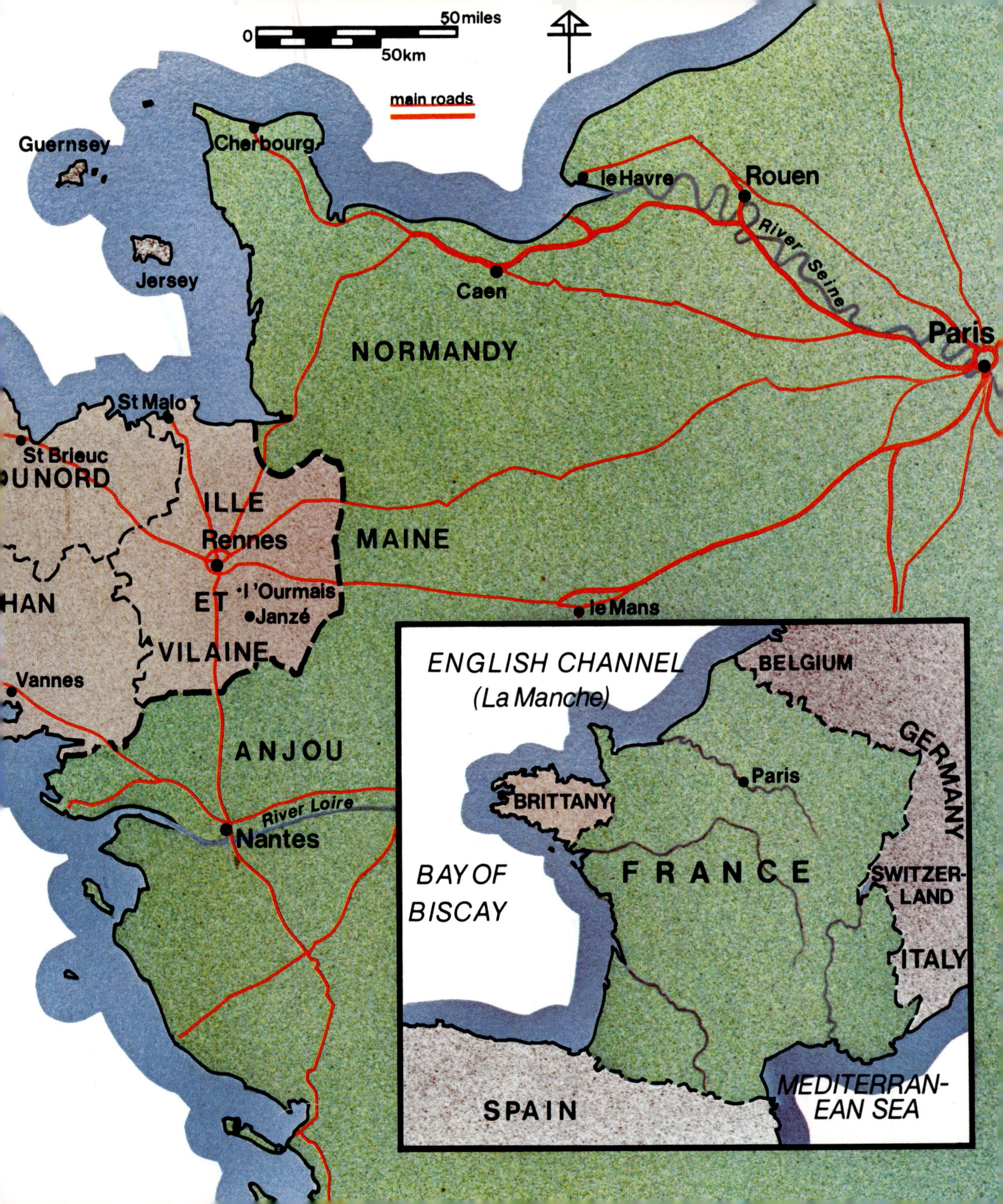
0
50 miles
50km
main roads
Guernsey
Jersey
Cherbourg
le Havre
Rouen
River Seine
Caen
Paris
NORMANDY
St Malo
St Brieuc
DUNORD
ILLE
Rennes
ET
VILAINE
HAN
l'Ourmais
Janzé
MAINE
le Mans
Vannes
ANJOU
River Loire
Nantes
ENGLISH CHANNEL
(La Manche)
BELGIUM
GERMANY
Paris
BRITTANY
FRANCE
SWITZER-LAND
ITALY
BAY OF BISCAY
SPAIN
MEDITERRAN-EAN SEA

Monsieur Gué lives with his wife, Madame Gué. They have two sons, Pascal, who is eight and Stéphane, who is ten. Their flat is on the fourteenth floor of a tower block. There is a very good view from the flat, but Madame Gué says she sometimes gets dizzy because it's so high up.

They live in a part of Rennes called Maurepas, about two and a half kilometres from the city-centre. It's a modern part of the city and is named after the nearby park of Maurepas.

Monsieur Gué is a postman. He works in the Colombiers post office. It's the largest post office in Rennes and more than 300 postmen work there. It takes Monsieur Gué about twenty minutes to bicycle to work and he has to be there by half past six in the morning!

Monsieur Gué usually works in the post office until nine o'clock. Then, he gets on his bicycle and sets off on his round. The letters are kept in leather panniers, strapped to his bike.

Monsieur Gué knows lots of people on his round. He often stops for a chat with the shopkeepers when he delivers their letters.

If he delivers the post to a block of flats, Monsieur Gué puts the letters in a box outside the main door. There is a different box for each flat.

Sometimes, Monsieur Gué has to deliver postal orders. He pays the money directly to the person whose name is on the postal order. Then he asks them to sign a special book to say that they have received the money. He carries the money in a leather bag which he must always wear over his shoulder.

By mid-morning, Monsieur Gué has delivered all the letters in his panniers. He stops at a special 'relay box' to collect the rest of the post for his round.

Monsieur Gué finishes his round at half past twelve. He goes back to the post office to sign off and then cycles slowly home.

It's lunch time, so the streets are very busy. Policemen blow their whistles and wave their arms to direct the traffic. Sometimes, a special 'concertina bus' rumbles past. These are bigger than ordinary buses, so they can carry more passengers in the rush hour.

Some of the most colourful parts of the city are pedestrian areas, where no traffic is allowed. People stroll up and down and look at all the shops. The Place de la Mairie is one of the busiest squares in Rennes. In the square, there are brightly coloured flower stalls where you can choose a bunch of flowers, wrapped in cellophane and golden ribbon.

There are cafés, too. If the weather is fine, people sit at tables outside and have a drink or something to eat.

Pascal and Stéphane wake up after their father has gone to work. On weekdays, they usually have coffee and bread for breakfast. They always drink from bowls in the morning. At weekends, Madame Gué makes hot chocolate and croissants, or 'pain au chocolat' – a kind of roll with a piece of chocolate in the middle.

School starts at half past eight in the morning. Pascal and Stéphane both go to the Saint Laurent primary school. It's just down the road, so they can walk there together.

This is Pascal's last year at primary school. Next year, he will go to the Lycée, or secondary school. There are 32 children in his class and their teacher, Madame Ségalen, is also the headmistress of the school.

Pascal's class elects a group of 'monitors' to keep the classroom clean and tidy. The monitors have a meeting every week. Pascal is the blackboard monitor. He leads today's meeting, but Madame Ségalen stays in the classroom to make sure it doesn't get too chaotic.

Madame Gué starts work as soon as the children have gone to school. Twice a week, she helps some friends with their fruit and vegetable stall at the market in Maurepas. It's early summer, so there are all kinds of fresh fruits and vegetables. The market is very busy. Madame Gué's stall is piled high with asparagus, green beans, fennel, artichokes and fruit such as cherries, strawberries and peaches.

When Madame Gué has finished work, she buys some food at the market and hurries home to make lunch. Pascal and Stéphane have their lunch break from half past eleven until one o'clock. They go home for lunch because they live so close by.

In France, lunch is the most important meal of the day and most people have a long lunch break. The Gué family usually have a six course lunch, including salad, cheese and dessert. The main course is fish or meat and they eat the vegetables as a separate course. At the end of the meal, they all drink real coffee.

After lunch, the boys have time to do some homework before they go back to school. Stéphane goes to his bedroom to practice the recorder. He has music lessons twice a week and the teacher always gives his class some tunes to play at home.

Pascal starts his maths homework. Maths isn't his favourite subject. He prefers writing stories, but he's not very good at French grammar!

Monsieur Gué has finished work for the day. In the afternoon, he does some odd jobs around the house. Some hooks in the bathroom need repairing. The bath looks very small because it has a built-in seat so you can sit down in the bath, or stand up to have a shower.

The family's bicycles need mending, too. Monsieur Gué repairs them all himself. Pascal helps when he gets home from school. He's learning to look after his own bike properly.

French children go to school on Saturday mornings and have Wednesday afternoons free. In winter, Pascal and Stéphane go ice-skating, or play football on Wednesday afternoons. Now that winter is over, they go swimming instead. The swimming pool is new and is built to look like a flying saucer!

On Saturday afternoon, Pascal and Stéphane help their mother with the shopping. Pascal goes to buy some bread for the evening meal. There is a lovely warm smell in the bakery. All kinds of bread of different shapes and sizes are sold there. Pascal buys a long stick of fresh white bread, called a baguette.

Stéphane and Madame Gué go to the Monoprix, the local supermarket. Madame Gué buys all her milk in litre bottles at the supermarket. In France, milk isn't delivered to your house.

Stéphane likes shopping at the market best of all. The stalls sell all kinds of different things: herbs; flowers; fresh meat and fish; sausage and pâté; fresh fruit and vegetables.

Some of the stalls sell live shellfish. Stéphane spends a long time watching the crabs scuttling around in their trays.

Further down the market-place, Madame Gué buys some cheese. There are small white goats' cheeses, boxes of Brie and huge slabs of Emmenthal. Camembert is one of the most popular kinds of cheese. It's creamy white inside, with a thick edible skin.

The Gué family are Catholics, like many other French people. On Saturday evening, they go to Mass at the Church of Saint Laurent. Their priest is called Father Jean. He and the people of Maurepas built the church themselves. It's built from stone, timber, mortar, glass and steel.

Father Jean is a great friend of the Gué family. After Mass, Monsieur and Madame Gué invite him round for supper and tell him what they have been doing during the week.

Sunday is a special day. It's Pascal's eleventh birthday. He has asked if they can go to the country to see his uncle Hamar, his aunt Thérèse and his two cousins, Sonia and Denis.

Monsieur Gué takes the car to the garage and buys some petrol. Then he loads up the car with fishing rods and baskets of food and they set off.

Uncle Hamar lives in a village called l'Ourmais, about 15 kilometres from Rennes. He is very proud of his house, which is 200 years old. When he bought the house, it was in a very bad state of repair. The family have done a lot of work on it but there is still a great deal to do.

Hamar was born in Algeria and came to France 15 years ago. He is a Muslim and Hamar is a Muslim name. His son, Denis, also has a Muslim name – Ali. Sometimes people get confused when they come to visit him, because he's called Denis at school and Ali at home.

Aunt Thérèse makes Breton galettes for lunch. Galettes are a kind of pancake. They can be eaten with almost anything – dipped in buttermilk, with ham and egg and mushrooms inside, or as a sweet with jam, stewed apples or honey.

After lunch, Hamar takes the children to see his rabbits. They're allowed to pick them up and stroke them. But Sonia and Denis know the rabbits are bred for eating, so they mustn't get too fond of them.

It's a warm sunny afternoon, so the Gué family walk down to the river Seiche to go fishing.

In summer, the family often take a picnic lunch and spend all day by the river. They catch all kinds of fish, but Monsieur Gué likes trout fishing best. Today, they only spend a few hours on the river bank, enjoying the sun and the water. Soon, it's time to go home. They want to get back in time for Pascal's birthday meal!

When they get home, Pascal and Stéphane help their mother to make supper. They are having a special meal, with all kinds of shellfish – crabs, prawns, shrimps, crayfish, oysters and tiny little sea snails. Pascal likes the snails. You fish them out of the shell with a pin and swallow them whole.

Stéphane asks if he can have a special meal on his birthday. Madame Gué says she will make one for him on his 'name day', in December. In France, a person's name day is as important as his birthday. French people are often named after saints, and each saint has a special feast day. Saint Stephen's day is on 26 December, so Stéphane celebrates his name day then.

At last, it's time for the birthday cake. It's a special cake, called a 'vacherin', made of blackcurrant ice-cream, meringue and fresh cream. There are eleven candles on the top. Pascal blows them all out at once and the rest of the family sing 'Joyeux Anniversaire', which means 'Happy Birthday' of course!